Sloth

Pride
Michael Eric Dyson

Envy
Joseph Epstein

Anger
Robert A. F. Thurman

Sloth
Wendy Wasserstein

Greed
Phyllis A. Tickle

Gluttony
Francine Prose

Lust
Simon Blackburn

For over a decade, The New York Public Library and Oxford University Press have annually invited a prominent figure in the arts and letters to give a series of lectures on a topic of his or her choice. Subsequently these lectures become the basis of a book jointly published by the Library and the Press. For 2002 and 2003 the two institutions asked seven noted writers, scholars, and critics to offer a "meditation on temptation" on one of the seven deadly sins. *Sloth* by Wendy Wasserstein is the sixth book from this lecture series. Previous books from The New York Public Library/Oxford University Press Lectures are:

Also by Wendy Wasserstein

Sloth

The Seven Deadly Sins

Wendy Wasserstein

The New York Public Library

2005

OXFORD
UNIVERSITY PRESS

Oxford   New York
Auckland   Bangkok   Buenos Aires   Cape Town   Chennai
Dar es Salaam   Delhi   Hong Kong   Istanbul   Karachi   Kolkata
Kuala Lumpur   Madrid   Melbourne   Mexico City   Mumbai   Nairobi
São Paulo   Shanghai   Taipei   Tokyo   Toronto

Published by Oxford University Press, Inc.
198 Madison Avenue, New York, New York, 10016
www.oup.com

Oxford is a registered trademark of Oxford University Press

Library of Congress Cataloging-in-Publication Data
Wasserstein, Wendy.
    Sloth / Wendy Wasserstein.
        p. cm.– (The Seven Deady Sins)
    ISBN-13: 978-0-19-516630-9
    ISBN-10: 0-19-516630-2

I. Laziness.
II. Title.
III. Series.

BF485/W38 2005
179'.8—dc22   2004007644

All original artwork © 2005 Serge Bloch / www.marlenaagency.com

Book design by planettheo.com

9 8 7 6 5 4 3 2 1
Printed in the United States of America
on acid-free paper

*For Michael Barakiva
and Jeremy Strong, Übersloths*

Contents

Editor's Note

This volume is part of a lecture and book series on the Seven Deadly Sins cosponsored by The New York Public Library and Oxford University Press. Our purpose was to invite scholars and writers to chart the ways we have approached and understood evil, one deadly sin at a time. Through both historical and contemporary explorations, each writer finds the conceptual and practical challenges that a deadly sin poses to spirituality, ethics, and everyday life.

The notion of the Seven Deadly Sins did not originate in the Bible. Sources identify early lists of transgressions classified in the fourth century by Evagrius of Pontus and then by John of Cassius. In the sixth century, Gregory the Great formulated the traditional seven. The sins were ranked by increasing severity, and judged to be the greatest offenses to the soul and the root of all other sins. As certain sins were subsumed into others and similar terms were used interchangeably according to theological review, the list evolved to include the seven as we know them: Pride, Greed, Lust, Envy, Gluttony, Anger, and Sloth. To counter these violations, Christian theologians classified the Seven Heavenly Virtues—the cardinal: Prudence, Temperance, Justice, Fortitude, and the theological: Faith, Hope, and Charity. The sins inspired medieval and

Renaissance writers including Chaucer, Dante, and Spenser, who personified the seven in rich and memorable characters. Depictions grew to include associated colors, animals, and punishments in hell for the deadly offenses. Through history, the famous list has emerged in theological and philosophical tracts, psychology, politics, social criticism, popular culture, and art and literature. Whether the deadly seven to you represent the most common human foibles or more serious spiritual shortcomings, they stir the imagination and evoke the inevitable question—what is *your* deadly sin?

Our contemporary fascination with these age-old sins, our struggle against or celebration of them, reveals as much about our continued desire to define human nature as it does about our divine aspirations. I hope that this book and its companions invite the reader to indulge in a similar reflection on vice, virtue, the spiritual, and the human.

Elda Rotor

Introduction

As long as I can remember, I have been searching for the right self-improvement plan. I always felt I was on the verge of finding happiness, if only I could lose weight, develop a better vocabulary in thirty days, have tighter abdominal muscles and buns, speak Spanish, achieve inner peace, schedule my day more efficiently, become more assertive, communicate more clearly, express the full range of my emotions, get a man to marry me in ten dates, get my daughter into Harvard at age twelve, understand the subtext of everything a man said, eat only organic produce, have the heart rate of a Rollerblader in South Beach, Florida, learn the joy of having sex in four hundred different positions and loving every one of them, find my inner child, renew my outer adult, come to terms with bad things happening to good people, embrace the Hebrew God, embrace the Christian God, embrace the Muslim God, and learn to write poetry like the actress Suzanne Somers.

I have followed endless self-improvement regimens. I have spent thousands of dollars on diet books, exercise books, cooking books, and spiritual guidance books. They always seem to be the answer for around three weeks, and then the system starts to unravel. For instance, when I first read *Dr. Atkins' Diet Revolution*,

I was thrilled with the possibility of living on bacon, eggs, and hunks of brie cheese. My mouth would water at the thought of thirty links of sausage for breakfast, and I could never imagine getting tired of saying, "Steak, again?" for dinner. But in the third week, I saw a piece of bread in a Bon Pain window and began uncontrollably weeping. I tried to break into the bakery, but the alarm went off and the fire department arrived. I went back to read Dr. Atkins for solace, and all I could find were anecdotes and lists related to this carb-free diet. In fact, if you read most diet books, there are only around two pages of the daily diet schedule, and the rest of the book is filled with inspirational affirmations on the new lifestyle.

After the bakery incident, I realized the key to change wasn't just dieting. To truly improve my life, I needed to become a better, more connected person. Therefore, I bought many manuals about relationships and communicating, and tried to really understand that men come from a different planet and acted accordingly. But thinking of men as aliens proved to be equally unsatisfying. I also tried to really communicate and express all my feelings. When I told my waiter at a Greek coffee shop that I was concerned about my potential for happiness and attributed it to a traumatic first grade experience, he didn't seem to be interested at all. Next, I really worked at becoming more assertive, and now none of my friends talk to me. Each time I looked to another guide for how to have a happier personal life, it only made me sadder and more isolated. I felt like everyone else was on the road to self-improvement and I wasn't. Lifestyle changes should be simple, the authors of these books swear daily on morning chat shows and infomercials, if only you follow their guidelines. But my life wasn't getting any better, and with each book, I became more and more defeated.

Having failed at improving my external life, I decided to focus on inner peace. If I couldn't learn to communicate, or eat only protein, then perhaps at least I could become singularly still. The more I concentrated on tranquility, however, the more nervous I became. The longer I visualized a stress-free life and the harmony of one, the harder it was for me to get to sleep at night. I couldn't align my shakras. I couldn't even maintain the downward dog! Instead, I stayed up all night trying to decode Linear A and Linear B, the only classical languages that have never been cracked. If I wasn't going to be stress-free, I figured I might as well become the most accomplished person I knew. I read *Wittgenstein for Dummies, Non-Euclidian Geometry for Dummies, Aramaic for Dummies, Berg Operas for Dummies, Descartes for Dummies, Post-Cold War Social Theory for Dummies, Defining the Absolute for Dummies, Writing Computer Viruses for Dummies, Genetic Cloning for Dummies,* and *Toward Peace in the Middle East for Dummies.* Although I mastered all of these, my daily life did not improve. I, frankly, knew too much, and it helped too little.

I was on the cusp of accepting myself and my life as the failure that it was when I went to visit my friend Pat Quinn in Los Angeles. Pat is a Hollywood talent agent, and I was hoping that her sense of purpose and drive would ignite my own. Driving along the freeways in Los Angeles is always comforting to me because I feel everyone is in his or her own isolated bubble. Even if they're listening to self-improvement tapes in their SUV Cadillacs, they're still driving back and forth on eight lanes of smoggy concrete. I find that reassuring.

Through Pat's inspiration, I decided I needed to get a grip on myself. There was one form of self-improvement I hadn't yet explored: bodybuilding. Even in midlife, I thought maybe I could become the next Mrs. Galaxy. And maybe after that, I could become governor of California. I liked the idea of firm muscles rippling on my arms and legs. I wanted to lift two-thousand-pound weights, because if I could do physical heavy lifting, surely I could lift myself up spiritually as well. So I went out to the mecca of body building—Venice Beach, California.

When I arrived at this supposed mecca, instead of finding my anticipated display of men and women pumping iron, I saw a seven-mile line of people leading to the Santa Monica pier. The people were a diverse assortment: all races, young, old, fat, thin, short, tall, beautiful, and ugly. As I approached them, I noticed the one thing they all had in common was that they were all carrying copies of a book titled *Sloth: And How to Get It.* The book had just been released, and since I had given up on self-improvement manuals, I was unaware of its publication. Apparently, on its first day in print, it had sold more copies than the Bible. My instinct was to ignore these hopefuls and begin my weight-lifting regimen. But the waiting throng appeared so enlightened that I decided to just get on line and see what the hoopla was.

I turned to a man standing next to me and asked, "What's everyone here for?" The man responded, "The most influential author of the world is here, the man who changed my life. I don't get up for anything anymore, but I came here to see him." "Who is he?" I asked. "The author of this book—*Sloth: And How to Get It,*" he answered. "I've tried everything, and this is the only one that's ever worked." I said, "I don't believe these kinds of books can change your life. And I've never heard of this one." The man on line explained, "You know, all these self-help books tell you what to do and how to do it and how much you should be doing of it. This is the only one that gives you permission not to be doing anything at all." I thought about that for a moment and found the idea to be overwhelmingly appealing. For someone who had spent her life aspiring to change, even the notion of not doing anything seemed revolutionary. I decided to take my place beside the pilgrims.

I waited days as the line wound up to the author. From what I understand, the progress of the line was impeded by the author's insistence on taking naps. When I finally reached him, he was lying on a hammock wearing light blue pajamas, the traditional sloth color. There were candy wrappers surrounding him, and he was watching a suspended plasma TV. I purchased a copy of his book from the bookseller standing beside him and handed it to the author for a signing. Instead of a traditional autograph, he had a rubber stamp with his signature on it. He looked at me and said only, "I can see sloth will really help you. You need this."

I knew he had seen into my inner, overscheduled soul. I went back to Pat's apartment, read the book, and it changed my life forever. I stayed in bed at Pat's house for a month, until she kicked me out and changed the locks. During that time, I gave myself over to sloth and have been practicing it ever since. It is the one lifestyle manual that I have been able to follow religiously. Even now, years later, I find that it just gets easier and easier.

Because of my success with sloth, and my extensive failure with other best-selling self-help manuals, the author asked me to write this introduction to the following new and revised edition. Also, he's too lazy to write it, and I respect that. So what follows is the original *Sloth: And How to Get It* plus a new chapter on the übersloths and a brand new activity-counting index.

Good luck! If you follow this book, I'm sure you will find the same happiness in total resignation that I have. Sloth gives us the courage to give up searching for self-improvement regimens. Read this book and you will say good-bye to all those naggy desires to better yourself. Sloth is the fastest-growing lifestyle movement in the world, and that's because it is completely doable. If you embrace sloth, it's the last thing you'll have ever have to do again.

Wendy Wasserstein
New York City

Sloth

And How to Get It

Revised Edition

PART ONE

Why Sloth Works

CHAPTER ONE

The Sloth Plan

Relax! Be happy! Let yourself go! This book will show you exactly how to do it. The Sloth Plan isn't an ordinary diet or exercise regimen. It's a philosophy that will change your entire life from this day onward.

I know many of you wake up to TV shows featuring women in white bikinis exercising on the beach in Hawaii. The Sloth Plan will confirm all your secret thoughts about them. These women are insane, overactive people who only eat grilled vegetables. They may live longer than any of us, but, remember, they have absolutely no depth.

Everyone who holds this book in hand has at some time made a New Year's resolution to get off the couch and join a gym.

People like Jack LaLanne and Arnold Schwarzenegger have made fortunes making every single reader of this book think there is something wrong with his or her horizontal instincts. Instead of eating cold pizza and beer for breakfast, we have all been led to believe we'd be better off lifting one- and two-hundred-pound slabs of iron in rotation. Have you ever been to a penal colony? That's what insane criminals are forced to do.

What's so great about the Sloth Plan, and why this plan is the fastest growing lifestyle change in the civilized world, is once you've got the idea, it can apply to every aspect of your life, not just exercise. Are you one of those supermoms who works all day, makes a delicious low-carb dinner for your family, does homework with your teenager, gives your husband a blowjob, and then stays up to do the dishes? Well, get ready to have the power to say to your kid "do your own homework" and to leave the dirty pots and pans for somebody else. Unfasten your seat belt, kiddo, because the Sloth Plan will, for the first time in your life, allow you to hang loose.

Forget about all the *shoulds* in your life. I *should* work harder, I *should* believe in God, I *should* make more money, I *should* get an erection, I *should* fit into a size four, I *should* have four children at Yale. The Sloth Plan says have the courage to look *should* in the face and say, "Go to hell! I'm not getting up for you!" And the energy you'll save by lying around and not fulfilling anyone's expectations,

even your own, will make you feel years younger. Everyone who has converted to the Sloth Plan is reenergized because, for the first time in their lives, they have the confidence to really rest.

As I said, the Sloth Plan is a complete lifestyle approach. The pounds lost stay lost forever because there is absolutely no good reason to get up. Think of it this way: Say you only ate low-fat protein for six months and went to spinning class every day. Yes, you would lose weight, but you would also be on such a tightly wound regimen that you would begin speaking constantly about your newfound health and nutrition. Friends would become so bored with your self-imposed regimen that they would begin to find you too self-involved to become intimate with. In other words, the low-fat, thigh-exercise diet would make you just plain flat. Sloth, on the other hand, is guaranteed to keep you well rounded. Followers of the Sloth Plan are never obsessed with their exercise schedule, because they are always resting. C'mon, tell me the truth. Who's sexier? A ninety-pound movie star on the Zone Diet or an Odalisque reclining.

Visualize, Through the Lens of a Sloth

Sloth works. If you don't believe me, let's start with a visualization.

All right. *First picture.* You've got your Palm Pilot in your hand with your schedule for the week:

5:30 A.M.	Get up.
6:00 A.M.	Walk for forty minutes.
7:00 A.M.	Feed the kids breakfast.
8:00 A.M.	Get kids to school.
9:00 A.M.	Arrive at the office.
10:00 A.M.	Morning staff meeting.

11:00 A.M.	Yoga break instead of coffee.
11:30 A.M.	Strategic planning meeting.
12:30 A.M.	Lunch with a client.
3:00 P.M.	Meeting with prospective client.
4:00 P.M.	Presentation.
5:00 P.M.	Twenty minutes of minute weight lifting.
5:30 P.M.	Teach the kids French.
6:00 P.M.	Bring all the kids to their psychiatrists.
7:00 P.M.	Braise a salmon.
9:00 P.M.	Attend a parent benefit committee.
10:30 P.M.	Attach yourself to a harness for unbelievable sex.
12:00 A.M.	Get in a taxi to tape CNN breaking news story about the election results.
2:00 A.M.	Moisturize Skin.
3:00 A.M.	Read and discuss online last week's issues of *The Economist*, *Time*, and *Hustler*.
4:00 A.M.	Sunrise semester, study Heidegger on cable television.
5:00 A.M.	Pilates.
5:30 A.M.	Start again.

Keep that in your head. And now here's my *second picture*:

Imagine yourself on a hammock for the entire day with only the breeze to move you. There's a plate of cheese (mostly double cream) on a nearby table, two large bottles of Diet Coke and wine.

A plasma TV hangs from one of the palm trees, and a clicker is neatly placed in your hand. Beside your hammock are master plot versions of *Vanity Fair*—both the Thackeray and the glossy magazine. Your only movement consists of crawling or rolling (more about the joys of rolling later), back into the living room or bedroom in case of inclement weather.

Now, which sounds like the happier, healthier, more humane way to live? Which picture depicts a person just out to prove something, and which one depicts someone finally at peace with his or her own universe? I promise after reading this book, following my careful exercise, diet, and life-control visualization plans, the second picture can be you. There is no reason to glow with health and achievement. Glowing takes work. From this moment on, I want you to have the will to say "no" to "glow." This is the twenty-first century. We are more than a century past the Victorians and the suffragettes. It is time to redefine human potential. It is time to embrace sloth.

Abandon Hope, All Ye Who Enter Sloth

I promise you the sloth approach is the most successful life-maintenance program. So many of us waste our time being angry at our bosses, our families, our president, or even our God. The Sloth Plan, on the other hand, helps us to accept that there is no real hope for change. Power is in the hands of an elite, entitled few, and there is no reason to waste our lives howling in the wilderness. In other words, we can become insane wolves or very happy, sleepy sheep. Sure, someone else is richer, thinner, and given a hell of a lot more chances because of who they know. But the hell with them. No matter how hard you try, it will never be an even playing field. I say put that sloth button on your chest and proudly go to bed instead.

Let me tell you a little story about Harry Ackerman. Harry was looking at high blood pressure, high blood sugar, depression, isolation, bankruptcy, divorce, and sexual perversion right in the face. Harry was at high risk for self-implosion. He went to shrinks, he went to career counselors, he went to hypnotists, he went to whores, he went to priests, he went to meditation clinics, he went to terrorist organizations, he went to the Marines, he even went to his mother. And only when Harry read this book did he figure anything out. As soon as Harry gave up, he finally felt positive again. Sloth cured Harry of being at risk, since Harry is now hardly being anything at all.

"The impact of sloth on my life has been overwhelmingly positive" says Harry from the roll-away bed he sleeps on at the Days Inn in Canton, Ohio. "I used to be afraid of everything. Now that I know there is nothing I have to do, I'm not afraid anymore. If something awful happens, the Sloth Plan has shown me how to ignore it. I feel positive for the first time in years."

The Sloth Mind-set

I want you to try to change your mind-set. We are trained since birth to want to "get up and go," and now it's killing us. The fashion and fitness industry is making a fortune on our collective self-hatred. Even the government prefers that we believe that exertion—both physical and spiritual—can change our lives. That's because the busier we are praying, exercising, or praying and exercising simultaneously, the less time we have to focus on them. The sloth mind-set says, "I've got nothing to prove and nowhere to go." There is no reason to be like the existential Sisyphus pushing that boulder up a mountain only for it to fall back again. Get real! Who really believes that life is like a movie, where someone born with a club foot can learn to ski for the gold in the Olympics? First of all, Olympic skiers burn out by age forty and become drunken ski instructors at two-star resorts in Gstaad. The sloth mind-set lets you know from the giddyap that the gladiators of the world are fine for entertainment, but they are no role models.

The Sloth Mantra

All right, enough preaching. When am I going to get to the diet? Where's the Sloth Plan I can laminate and carry around in my pocket? Here are the principles you need to remember, and I made it easy for you. As you will see, this book will make *everything* easy for you because we want you to stop making an effort right now. Think S L O T H literally and you will always have our five commandments nearby. (You see, we've even cut the commandments in half!)

1. S Sit instead of stand. There is no reason to get up for anything. Everything can come to you. That includes food, sex, religion, conversation, intellectual stimulation, even freedom.
2. L Let yourself go. Say goodbye to everything that keeps you tightly wound. Start today by throwing away your Palm Pilot, Blackberry, and for those of you who are electronically challenged, your Filofax.
3. O Open your mouth and let anything you feel like enter. Once you stop restricting intake, food will become more pleasurable and less of a neurotic compulsion.
4. T Toil no more. For god's sake, stop working unless it is something you can do lying down.
5. H Happiness is within me. I don't have to work at it. And happiness, not annual checkups and vitamin B-12 shots and Viagra, is the key for a permanent groundwork for disease prevention.

Again, for those of you who need constant visual reinforcement or want to change the prayer in your mezuzah, here is the sloth mantra.

SLOTH

S   Sit instead of stand.

L   Let yourself go.

O   Open your mouth.

T   Toil no more.

H   Happiness is within me.

I promise these five sloth commandments will change your life like no other plan you have tried before. It's time to stop looking for answers. The answer is sloth.

CHAPTER TWO

A Personal History

Okay. I know what you naysayers are thinking. Why the hell should you listen to me? Who the hell am I? What are my credentials? Am I another quack just out there to make a buck?

I Am a Regular Guy

I am not a trained medical doctor. But I have had medical problems, so I know about all the latest medical advances. I am also not an ordained minister or priest. But I have had sex with underage boys and girls, which gives me a holiness equivalency degree. Finally, I am not a nutritionist or an exercise guru. However, I did work as a waiter at the Brussels Restaurant in Covent Garden where I placed mussels and french fries onto a conveyor belt.

I have no interest in becoming a national celebrity or infomercial host. Believe you me, I've been asked to make a sloth anti-motivational tape to compete with those Kung Fu kickboxing videos. As far as I'm concerned, all those men pumped up with steroids who sell portable ab machines on late-night television should be shot with Dramamine.

Trust me. I am just a regular guy whose life was totally changed by sloth, and I am on a mission to make sloth possible for all of you.

Now you might ask, how can anyone who is truly a sloth become a crusader? First of all, I wrote this book entirely lying down. Second of all, I dictated half of it and my assistant made up the other half. And most importantly, I have never said that the sloth has no desire to make easy money. I know that lifestyle and dieting books are taking over the publishing industry, even at the revered Oxford University Press, so why shouldn't I make an easy few million? Christ, it's not like I'm wasting my time writing a first novel that will only sell two thousand copies. Sloths are not stupid. If Suzanne Somers can make a fortune from her diet book or whoever the hell wrote *The Zone* then why shouldn't I? Come on, wouldn't you like the royalties of whoever wrote the *South Beach Diet*? It makes a lot more sense than, say, writing poetry, academic criticism, or—god forbid—plays. Those things take genuine work, and the monetary rewards are generally not commensurate.

But if you still don't trust my genuine instincts, let me fill you in on my family story.

My Father, the Anti-sloth

My father came to this country in 1922. His is a tale of twentieth century anti-sloth America. His is a story of initiative, ingenuity, and American get-up-and-go.

My father landed on Ellis Island from Vlosk, Russia, with his sister Natalia. His mother died on the boat from an undiagnosed appendicitis, and his father had left them earlier for a singer in Vienna.

When my father arrived he was only eight years old, and his sister was twelve. They went to live with their cousin Hinda, who was a stenographer at the International Ladies Garment Workers Union. My father's sister became a communist rabble-rouser. She was going to change the world.

My father, who could never even imagine sloth, bussed tables at Ratners, shined shoes on Wall Street, and even took tickets at a movie theater. At the same time he managed to become first in his class at Washington Irving High School.

For my father, America was a land of opportunity. Sure, there was an elite class and clubs to which he'd never belong. But he believed if he worked hard and did his share, he could have a good life.

And then the Depression came. My father had better grades than sons of senators, lawyers, and presidents who went to Harvard, Yale, and Princeton, but these institutions weren't looking for diversity in those days. Since the Ivy League was a well-endowed gentleman's club, my father didn't go to college.

My father knew that in times of trouble people need to be entertained. From his early days taking tickets at the Brooklyn Paramount and RKO, he had mastered the art of putting on a show. He had a great sense of humor—a laugh a second. On the other hand, my father's sister became increasingly dour. She developed a crush on Stalin and kept a large photo of him in a heart frame beside her tiny cot bed. My father even found diary entries on how much my aunt would have liked to lick Stalin's moustache.

With money from the tips he had made from shining shoes, my father bought a train ticket to Los Angeles. The day he got there he passed a shantytown where homeless dreamers lived. He even thought he recognized one or two silent film stars.

My father immediately got a job delivering chocolate for See's candy store. He was also sweeping the floors at Max Factor, the makeup impresario, and taking inventory of lingerie at Frederick's of Hollywood. My father was a smart man but not an introspective one. If he felt a tinge of envy, bitterness, or even isolation, he just worked some more.

One day when he was delivering See's chocolates to Ginger Rogers's dog walker in *The Gay Divorcée*, he noticed that the twin Pekinese were walking out of step. My father immediately offered to take their leash, and the dogs began doing time steps. Ginger fired her dog walker on the spot and hired my father.

The rest was history. All those Astaire and Rogers films were actually choreographed, written, and directed by my father. I know there are names like Hermés Pan and Donald Ogden Stewart on the credits, but secretly, it was my father who really conceived and danced the Continental. Sure, it looks like Fred Astaire, but my father had transformational gifts. He was interested in power—not personal recognition. He always used a pseudonym.

My father, who slept only two hours a night, became president of Fox, Paramount, and MGM. He also became the anonymous president of See's chocolates, Max Factor makeup, and the Beverly Wilshire Hotel. While his sister remained on her cot underneath the photo of Stalin, my father became more and more anticommunist. In fact, he gave his sister's name to the House Un-American Activities Committee. To him, even

Mickey Mouse wasn't enough of a capitalist. In my father's eyes, anyone who made under twenty million dollars a year was an out-and-out sloth. My father's dream was to send John Wayne to the home of any American who was napping and toss him out of bed. He didn't believe in national health insurance, welfare, or social security. He believed in the inalienable right to personal initiative.

The Carpe Diem Anti-sloth Movement was started by my father four years before he died. The Movement funds all media, print, and video advertising that reminds you that your life is inadequate. The subliminal message is you should and could be richer, thinner, happier, and holier. The Carpe Diem funds the Home Network, the Health Network, the God Network, and every other self-improvement network.

When my father died, he left his entire fortune to the Anti-sloth campaign. On my father's behalf, I must say that his bequest was color-blind. He would fund anyone and anything with get-up-and-go except for me. I had to make it on my own.

Let It All Go

Being an introspective man, I could have responded to my father's life and legacy in two ways. I could have taken an angry "I'll show him" approach and spent my life overachieving and proving that I could never live up to his standards. Or I could let it all go. Get out of the race. Take a back seat to life and declare "I've got this all figured out, and I'm getting out." The day I chose the latter was a turning point in my life. I remember it as if it were yesterday. It was my senior year at college. To make up for my father's lack of formal education, I was getting a joint degree from Harvard, Princeton, and Yale. I was Phi Beta Kappa at all three, plus I was on the squash team at Harvard, the swim team at Princeton, and president of the Yale Dramat. One spring day, I was on my way to Skull and Bones, my secret society, when a friend happened to ask me what sex I was. Frankly, I had been so busy all my life that I hadn't noticed. I played sports on both men's and women's teams, and I had also danced the young male and female lead in the New York City Ballet's *Nutcracker.* In high school I had dated both men and women and was currently in deep and serious relationships with both. As far as I was concerned, I was going to be a father and a mother, and when I ran for president I would have a charming First Lady at my side and be escorted by a poet laureate husband. Truly, I had never considered the sexual-identity issue. Gender courses were something sophomores who would have low-ranked academic careers paid attention to. For the first time in my life I was stumped. I remember I sat down in the middle of the New Haven Green and began to cry. And I sat and cried for the next three months. Friends brought me food while student tour guides pointed me out to parents. My father sent the entire Mayo Clinic and a forklift to remove me, but I would not budge. I began to sing. "We shall not / We shall not be moved. / Just like a tree who stands beside the border / We shall not be moved." After six months the moving company Nice Jewish Boy with a Truck came to remove me. I went only because the nice Jewish boy said his mother would feed me chicken soup, and I had never had a Jewish mother. When I moved in with Mrs. Friedlander my father cut me out of his life. The last time I saw him was on TV. He was being interviewed by Charlie Rose, when he referred to me on that broadcast as "My son, the sloth." According to legend, on the day he died he was screaming, "Don't make me rest! Don't make me rest!"

Indolence Is Bliss

Since my epiphany at Yale, I have devoted my life to perfecting the art of sloth. Before I found sloth, I was an angry, driven, competitive young man. Now I am content in my own blasé oblivion. I have found my way to cluttered unconsciousness—and you can too. In all honesty, not only am I a happy man now but I don't give a damn about what's going on in anyone else's backyard. Sloth looks at all the rules and says, "No, thank you." And *that*, ladies and gentlemen, is the greatest gift you can give yourself.

And now for a little history of sloth. After all, you don't have to believe me just because of my life story. My theories are intellectually sound. I am, as I said, a graduate of Harvard, Princeton, and Yale.

CHAPTER THREE

The Concise History of Sloth

I don't want any of you to think that I have come to the Sloth Philosophy without knowing its background. I may be lying on my back, but I can still read. I have done, in fact, extensive research of not only sloth but all seven deadly sins. To prove to those of you who think this is yet another lifestyle revolution that will come and go, I will now provide you with a concise history of sloth. Unlike the fat-free fad or Pilates, sloth has been around for more than a thousand years.

So you want to know who was responsible for the seven deadly sins? Well, first of all, you're asking the wrong question. It was originally eight deadly sins, and they were collated by Evagrius of Pontus, a fourth-century monastic theologian. Evagrius, who I liked to called Eva, migrated from Asia Minor to Egypt, where he spent his life examining the spiritual crises presented in the Bible. (Look, someone's got to do it, and usually it's best when they're from Asia Minor.) For those of you interested in gossip, there's an interesting side note about Eva. He was once tempted by an affair, and his impetus for fleeing Asia Minor was to remove himself from the source of the temptation. In a later chapter, I will dwell on how full immersion into the sloth philosophy can help anyone (a monastic theologian or a raving nymphomaniac) avoid temptation, because it's just too difficult to move.

The Eight Deadly Sins

Evagrius's list of eight sins included the following:

- Gluttony
- Lust
- Avarice
- Sadness

- Anger
- Acedia
- Vainglory
- Pride

The order here is not haphazard—Evagrius's list is compiled in increasing severity. The criteria for how sinful a sin really is determined by the extent to which it fixates on the self—so gluttony, which is about intake, is considered to be the least evil of the sins, while pride, which glorifies the existing self, is considered the worst.

(Excuse me, while I take a break. I'm not used to this kind of mental exertion. Remember—I'm doing this all for you, and you should be grateful—I've already come to my life conclusions.)

In the sixth century, Pope Gregory consolidated the sins into seven. In other words, he eliminated "vainglory" and "acedia" because of their respective similarities to "pride" and "sadness." He also added envy, as its own sin. Pope Gregory's list of sins, as presented in his *Moralia In Job,* was pride, envy, anger, sadness, avarice, gluttony, and lust. And, in all honesty, they sound a lot more like most of my friends than Evagrius's list. I mean, when you think about the people you know, would you really say, "I can't bear him—he's so vainglorious!" As opposed to Evagrius's list, Pope Gregory's started with the most serious of sins and went to the least. In his worldview, sin was measured by the degree to which it prevented a human from feeling love for God.

Laziness = Holiness

My point to Pope Gregory would have been that it takes energy to sin. You have to get up pretty early in the morning to have avarice, lust, or even pride. If we just remained in the comfort and safety of our beds, perhaps we would all be holier men. It is true that during the Middle Ages, some of the greatest churches and cathedrals in the world were built. But simultaneously, the organized industrious adulation of God led to its own undermining, epitomized in the Protestant Reformation of the sixteenth century.

There have been two major changes to the list of sins after Pope Gregory's updating in the sixth century. St. Thomas Aquinas destroyed the notion that certain deadly sins were deadlier than others. Unlike Evagrius and Pope Gregory, St. Thomas Aquinas believed that all of these sins were equally likely to lead you straight to hell. Frankly, I don't get how being sad in your living room can possibly be as bad as sleeping with your neighbor's wife (which, by the way, I have done on a number of occasions, before I became a full-time sloth). For Aquinas, the sin of sadness was spiritual, not physical. The laziest girl in his town was just too lethargic to embrace God or *any* good work in God's name. Finally, complaints that "sadness" was too vague to be a sin led the Church to replace it with "sloth" in the seventeenth century.

The Virtue of Sadness

Eight hundred years of Christian theological thought led the sin of "sadness" to evolve into "sloth." Interesting then, that deep emotions, which we now go on talk shows like *Oprah* to express, were considered a sin. Thomas Aquinas noted that this sadness, or "acedia," usually hit the monks at around 4 P.M. Any savvy internist could tell you that at 4 P.M., monks who were living on a diet of their own bread and honey would suffer from acute low blood sugar. Any modern psychiatrist wouldn't dare say that sadness is a sin. Sadness is just a reason to buy low-priced Prozac and other antidepressants on the Internet.

The Sloth Crawleth

And what about the actual animal, the sloth itself? Why isn't our sluggish sin named pig or fat cat? When you consider that the contents of a well-fed sloth's stomach constitute almost two-thirds of its entire body mass, you can't help but be impressed by how much food these creatures can consume. Even a camel's hump can't possibly be two-thirds of its body weight. And yet, sloths live only on leaves. It's a very focused, and not very curious, diet. The leaves provide little energy, and appropriately, sloths expend even less. Sloths usually eat, sleep, and even give birth while hanging from limbs by their specialized long, curved hand-claws. They can spend up to one entire week without standing upright. I've tried to do that, but I only make it to five days.

Inertia

Sloths have no defenses. They are not aggressive animals. They are happy to spend their time camouflaged in trees and seldom even hit the ground. Even a mama sloth can rarely be persuaded to descend and pick up a baby sloth who has fallen. Although this usually results in the baby sloth's death, the mama sloth knows better than to get up. Remaining inert is the animal's highest priority.

I have found a text by a monk, Benedictum Benedix, whose sister's wife's cousin once met Thomas Aquinas. Benedictum Benedix wrote a parable called "The Eager Beaver and the Sloth." I'm going to share it with you now.

The Eager Beaver and The Sloth

There once was an Eager Beaver who lived underneath Chartres. And everyday the beaver said to himself, "What can I do to make myself a holier beaver?" Every day, he built another dam in honor of God. Every day, he ferreted a hole toward the main sanctuary, so that he could be closer to God. He worked and worked. On a tree beside the cathedral, lived a sloth who never moved. The sloth sucked the leaves of the tree as thousands of pilgrims came to Chartres. And every day, the Beaver came to look at the Sloth and say to him, "I look at you, and I want to move. I want to build. I want to praise God. I want to create. Your example gives me the energy to go on." So the Beaver gnawed and gnawed a tunnel until he came into the Great Hall at Chartres. And on the day he finally arrived in the sanctuary, a Mother Superior saw him, screamed, and he was immediately trapped. As the lowliest monk took him away in a paper bag, the Sloth watched from his tree. "Holy Beaver!" the Sloth explained. "You can't take him away." And the monk looked at the Sloth and disregarded him: "You know nothing of holiness. Go suck a leaf!" The Beaver was drowned in a lake that he himself had damned, as an act of homage to God. And as the water filled the Eager Beaver's body, he thought to himself, "I wish I were more like the Sloth. The Sloth, and not God, holds the key to life."

When Thomas Aquinas found his sister's wife's cousin's parable, he burned it immediately. But what he didn't know was that one copy remained in the gift shop at Chartres. And that is where I found it. I have shown it to other scholars, who disregard it and say that I fabricated both it and its author. But I say to them, I'm far too lazy to fabricate anything. Therefore it must be true.

What's the Point?

The meaning of the Benedictum Benedix parable is clear. Sometimes bad things happen to good people, or good little beavers. The amount of work you do, or how eager a beaver you are, is not going to change that. The Beaver, who spent his whole life trying to get close to God, was eventually executed by His servants. The Sloth, whose talking to the guard on behalf of the Beaver was the most active he had been for years, got to live happily ever after. You can understand why Thomas Aquinas felt compelled to burn this story. It was antithetical to his brand of holiness.

Join the Movement!

In the nineteenth century, sloth became not only a sin against God but also a sin against capitalism and the Industrial Revolution. Think of it this way, an Industrial Revolution required industrious

people. An Age of Invention demanded those who were willing to invent. Although machines were meant to reduce the workload, in fact they made more work possible.

When the Pilgrims landed on Plymouth Rock in Massachusetts, they were compelled to found a new country that assured them freedom of religion and freedom from sloth. The underlying rights of Americans are to life, liberty, and the pursuit of happiness. The pursuit of anything takes some original thought and gumption. America was a new world, in which inheritance and class were not necessary for success. Far more important was good old-fashioned perseverance.

American society has evolved from the days of earnest Puritanism. On the cusp of the new millennium, America is home to the fastest growing Sloth movement in the world. And with this book, I want to help you join this movement. In the pages that follow, I will detail for you how to become a sloth in your diet, exercise, work, and even love life. Isn't it time we move forward from the precepts of the Puritans and Thomas Aquinas? This is the twenty-first century. Isn't it time we look to the personal contentment of the sloth?

CHAPTER FOUR

Sloth Will Change Your Life

You will succeed with sloth. Sloth will change the way you look at your body and your life. Sloth will help you stop binge eating because you can eat all the time. You can learn to manage your cravings because it takes effort to have cravings. It is impossible to be slothful and have pride or even lust. Pride requires some ambition, and with sloth, ambition becomes a thing of the past. Consider yourself on permanent vacation.

The Three Types

I like to divide those whom sloth can potentially save into three categories.

Category One: Do you ever hear someone say, *"I rest all the time, but I'm always tired."* Believe you me, this person never rests. They may be lying down, but they are thinking, "I should be exercising, I should be reading, I should be having sex with my neighbor, I should be making more money, I should be talking to my children about their drug habits." This chronically tired person is an ideal candidate for sloth. By adopting a slothlike lifestyle they will, for the first time in their lives, be truly rested.

Category Two: *"I don't need to rest—I get high on life."* This is bologna if I ever heard it. Who could possibly get high on life? In life, there is disease, random acts of violence, natural disasters, undisclosed fascist governments, not to mention world poverty and hunger. If you look life in the face, you couldn't possibly get high on it. Even love fades. Once you adopt sloth, you are dealing with a responsible reaction to the truth about living.

Category Three: Here's my favorite—the fellow who says, *"There are certain things I just have to do."* Like what? See the Eiffel Tower? I say watch the Travel Network. Have sex with Britney Spears? Watching her video from the comfort of your living room is a nearly identical experience. Visit your mother before she dies? Buddy, if you haven't been kind to your mother all your life, this final visit isn't going to make it up to her. And for those of you who *need* to become CEOs of companies, isn't it better to avoid the inevitable temptation of graft and income tax evasion? Look at our friends from Enron—they could've benefited from a little sloth.

Of course, I know what your next question is. You're beginning to see it from my point of view. You're beginning to think, "Yes, he's right! But how do I get there? Where do I begin? It can't be as simple as that." But it is.

The Simplicity of Sloth

Let me explain to you, before I give you the sloth behavioral diet, about some simple scientific facts.

Understanding the Importance of Lethargiosis

A scientific phenomenon called "lethargiosis"—the process of eliminating energy and drive—is the first vital step in becoming a sloth. By burning ambition instead of feeding on it, lethargiosis breaks the cycle of excess energy and stored dreams. For those of you who are not medical doctors, let me explain this phenomenon to you a little more clearly. Everyday activities provide us with little hopes and dreams on which our body feeds. It makes it possible to wake up the next morning. For instance, if we've learned or experienced something new, we want to try it again and learn even more. That's the insidious way children's television works. Or, on more personal terms, if we've met somebody we're attracted to, we might want to see them again. Our interest is engaged by an ongoing saga in the workplace or in the continuing development of our children. Because we feed on little carrots of curiosity and hope, we don't dwell on the futility of our larger dreams and goals. It's easier to think about the person who works down the cubicle from you than to focus on whether or not career fulfillment is possible.

When we deprive ourselves of all activity, we have no little, everyday goals to fixate on. Our imagination then, has to jump to the big stuff, and this is when you've entered lethargiosis. After a few weeks of devouring your grand dreams, your imagination reaches a state of emptiness and becomes void of ambition. This is when you know lethargiosis has been successful—because there is absolutely no reason, big or small, to get up. You emerge from lethargiosis a true and complete sloth.

Lethargiosis versus Tranquility

Warning! Do not mistake lethargiosis for a meditative trance. Meditation takes work and is an enforced form of tranquility.

Lethargiosis is not a state of tranquility, it is a state of pointlessness. Meditation requires a tidy, methodical mind capable of entering a trance because of the ridiculousness of repetition. Sloth is in no way methodical. In fact, it is the antimethod. The state of lethargiosis is not a trance but an enervated limp.

Top Ten Lies about Sloth

Before we go on to the actual sloth life plan, I want to recognize those readers who are having doubts. I am aware of your criticisms and will be happy to list them, but I simply do not have the energy to refute them. Here is a list of the top ten lies about sloths:

1. Sloth is dangerous and causes a variety of medical problems.
2. Sloth causes you to gain weight. (Remember, even eating requires an amount of energy that the sloth isn't willing to expend.)
3. A sloth life is unbalanced and deficient in human interaction.
4. A sloth lifestyle may cause people to feel tired and weak, and will increase blood pressure.
5. Sloth is an anticapitalist conspiracy.
6. Humans are meant to live in the vertical, not horizontal, position.
7. Lethargiosis causes bad breath. (Only in dogs.)

8. Sloth causes constipation.
9. Sloth leads to mental atrophy.
10. Sloth will lead to the end of democracy and civilization.

To all of these lies, I say no one ever went to war because they were sloths. No one was ever murdered or killed in the name of sloth. Furthermore, sloths don't go on religious crusades. Terrorism requires initiative and cunning. If sloths are fundamentalists, their fundamentalist belief is to rest. Hate takes energy. Destroying the ozone layer requires industry. Therefore, slothdom can save humanity.

In Part Two, I will give you an exact plan on how to begin to sloth today—and for life.

How to Do It

CHAPTER FIVE

Success with Sloth

Cleaning Up

A great deal of your success with the Sloth Plan is based on how well you prepare for it. You need to clear your personal life, professional life, and physical life of any and all previous entanglements. I understand that this sounds difficult, but I will help you.

Personal Life

Sever all ties. I know those of you who are family men and women, and are deeply involved in the lives of spouses and children, will say, "But I have to be there to pick Johnny up from school," or "I have to see Cindy play soccer," or "I have to make dinner for Joe," or "I have to have sex with Selma otherwise she'll leave me." My answer for all of you is to get your loved ones on your team. Tell them that what you're about to do is going to give you a happier, healthier, longer life. If they truly love you, they will want to keep you around and will support you in this endeavor. If, on the other hand, your spouse is completely reliant on your income, cooking, or sexual favors, who the hell needs them, anyway? Wouldn't your children be better off learning to separate? Isn't it time for you to stop enabling their dependency on you? Think about it this way. One sloth in a household can often inspire the rest of the family to join in this revolutionary lifestyle. I'll give you an example. Once one von Trapp began singing, the rest couldn't help but join along. Of course, between their singing and their fleeing Nazi-occupied Austria, the von Trapps do represent the anti-sloths. But the point is, once they hiked across the Alps and got to Vermont, why couldn't they relax a little instead of opening that ridiculous inn? Similarly, one inspirational sloth can lead his or her entire family to abandoning all structure and futile regimen. A family that sloths together stays together.

Professional Life

Professional life is a little trickier. It is possible to be a sloth and stay economically solvent with a laptop computer. There is a growing world of cybersloths and, for that matter, cybersloth gear. For instance, my latest catalog includes voice-activated software that eliminates the need to actually press keys, self-cleaning pajamas that do not require laundering, and food that cooks itself by your table.

Most importantly, before you can truly sloth, you must cancel all appointments. People can come to you, as long as they don't make you stand on ceremony—or anything else. And, you can't have any deadlines, since you couldn't possibly be expected to meet them. In order to achieve lethargiosis, you must force yourself to do absolutely nothing for the two-week induction period in order to purge your system of all the labor-related impulses that have been implanted by society. Once you emerge from lethargiosis, you can be productive if you want to, but only if you want to, on your own terms, and with no external expectation. By the way, you might want to look at your investments every now and then in order to support your slothdom, and to pay me my consulting fee, which you can do by reaching me on my website, www.sloth.org.com.edu.

Physical Life

Do not listen to any doctors. Doctors are quacks. They will tell you you need exercise. They will tell you you have high blood pressure. They will tell you you have to limit your intake of fats, your intake of proteins, your intake of carbohydrates, and your intake of sugar, alcohol, and tobacco. Every doctor is on the payroll of pharmaceutical conglomerates. It might be the organic pharmaceutical conglomerates, the Eastern medical pharmaceutical conglomerates, or the Merck corporation, but they are all getting kickbacks.

It is in a doctor's interest to eliminate sloths so that you will continue to come to their offices. It's also in their interest to create parasitic relationships. How many of you receive anonymous e-mails to buy discount Viagra? Every single one of those e-mails was sent by members of the medical establishment. If you adopt the sloth lifestyle, you can delete every one of those e-mails today. The American Medical Association (AMA) invented depression. When they eliminated shock treatment as the prime method for treating acute depression, they did it because they knew they could hook more patients on Prozac, Zoloft, and whatever they'll come up with next.

Doctors are also on the payroll of health clubs, hotels, cruise ships, and Korean fruit markets. They are involved in an international conspiracy to make you believe that you can improve your life by consulting them and by buying their products. Sloth will eliminate the medical profession from your life. I want you—right now—to throw away every blood pressure medication, every antidepressant, every thyroid pill, every antibiotic, every antacid, antihistamine, sexual enhancer, and mood-altering medication. You won't need any of them with sloth.

Dig In

Once you've done the necessary cleaning up, it is important to set up your nest. Be sure you have a comfortable couch indoors, or hammock outdoors. I like a goose-down pillow, but if you're a rubber-foam sort of person, go right ahead and be my guest. For those of you in colder climates, I suggest a down comforter or maybe something with a thermal lining.

Key Ingredients

A low side table should be placed within arm's reach for food and other necessities. I suggest a nonperishable box of triple-cream Oreo cookies, Cheetos, Salt 'n' Vinegar potato chips, dried apricots, raisins, and cashew nuts for protein. You can drink as much alcohol

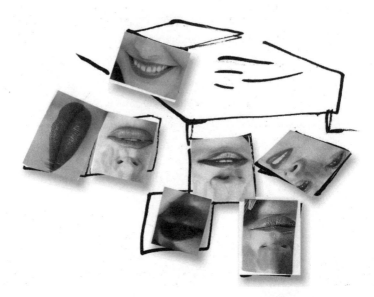

as you want, but be careful of consuming too much liquid, which will result in repeated trips to the bathroom. Those trips can become too exhausting for a sloth. Remember, it's doctors who say you have to drink eight glasses of water a day. I like to keep stacks and stacks of magazines on my bed, but again, be careful not to tangle with any urgent news. Pictures are preferable to text. For instance, I take great solace in Jennifer Aniston and Brad Pitt's marriage, and the changing status of their hairdos. Some sloths enjoy having a large plasma TV hanging near their resting place. I suggest one that goes immediately to the cartoon network, with easy access to MTV, the Roseanne reruns on Nickelodeon, and I have to admit that I have a big crush on Charlie Rose. Also, let me state that I do nothing about this crush—I do not act on it in any way. That would be anti-slothful of me. And furthermore, I turn the sound off when Charlie is interviewing anyone who could possibly make me want to become active.

Take Your Measurements

Finally, take your measurements. As the amount of activity you perform plummets, you'll be surprised at how little food you need to survive. Even with that carefully prepared low table close by, you will tire of triple-cream Oreos. I know it sounds impossible, but it's true. Taking your measurements, or better yet having someone else take them, will prove to you that you are on the right track.

ALL RIGHT!

READY . . . SET . . . SLOTH!

CHAPTER SIX

Welcome to Your Inner Sloth

The Induction Period

You are now ready to begin the sloth lifestyle. For the first two weeks, you must be very careful to follow all our rules or lethargiosis will not set in. There must be no cheating, or I will personally come to your house to reprimand you, and you now know how much I despise getting up. I promise the sloth lifestyle will work, but only if you make the commitment. You can be a sloth in every part of your life, except to the following rules:

THE TEN RULES OF SLOTH

1. **Do not clean up.** Forget everything you ever learned in nursery school about putting your toys away. Putting something away creates double work, because you'll only need to take it out again next time you need it. The more accessible everything is, the easier your life will be. From now on, think of mess as creative and even entertaining. There is no such thing as a garbage pail. The right place for a candy wrapper is on the floor.

2. **Do not wash.** We live in an environmentally challenged society because we are obsessed with bathing. There really is no need to shower every day. All it does is deplete the rain forest and your body of essential moistures and oils. In fact, it has been proven that shampooing every day strips your hair of body, gloss, and natural colors. Bathe only when you feel like you're on the verge of contracting something unpleasant, like mold or ringworm. I don't have anything against mold or ringworm per se, but their presence can lead to doctor's appointments, and you know what I think about them.

3. **Learn to love yourself as you are.** Believe me, you're not going to be any better or any happier if you lose forty pounds, if you learn to speak French, or read *Ulysses*. I've read *Ulysses*

and *Finnegan's Wake* before I found sloth and I was still miserable. And no one learns to speak French as well as someone who was born in France, and every Frenchman would be happy to tell you that. As for weight loss, it's a hopeless seesaw of ups and downs. Jenny Craig or any other weight-loss guru couldn't care less if you're fat or thin, as long as you pay a big fat initiation fee. And believe me, nobody's weight or blood-pressure count is listed in their obituary.

4. **Stop competing.** Motivation is spurred on by competition. In other words, we often do a job we're not necessarily interested in just because we want to do better than the person sitting next to us. Forget about whoever's sitting next to you. Forget that your sister married a man worth a hundred million dollars. Forget that your best friend looks thirty years younger than you do. Forget that everyone else's children have gotten into college and your son is stealing hubcaps. The real money is in the hands of a few, and most likely, it's not going to be you. So why bother competing, since inevitably you'll only get a miniscule, unsatisfactory piece of the pie.

     Yes, there are people like Oprah Winfrey who pulled themselves up by their bootstraps to have stunning success, but do you know whether or not she's really a human being? Do you know if she's ever had a single moment of joyous sloth in her life? I, personally, doubt it. My advice to all of you is turn your switch off while you can. If Oprah had to turn her switch off—if she had to give up her show, her diet, her schedule, her assistants—I am convinced she wouldn't know what the hell to do with herself. She would be void. In a world where two jet planes can destroy the World Trade Center, isn't confronting the underlying emptiness the only way to survive?

5. **Food is no longer an issue**. I know I mentioned keeping triple-cream Oreos at your bedside, plus dried apricots and nuts. But that is the long-term goal. In your first two weeks, I don't give a damn how much you eat, and neither should you. Have whatever you want. In Susan Orbach's seminal book, *Fat is a Feminist Issue*, she urged her dieters to fill their houses with the foods they craved most (ice cream, halvah, chocolate-chip cookies, triple-cream cheeses . . .) and demythologize them. In other words, she urged her people to confront their secret food fantasies. I don't personally believe in feminism or dieting, but as I believe that there are no limits, you will be satiated and eventually the cravings will stop. It's difficult to continue to lust for a brownie hot-fudge sundae and pizza, when they are always available.

6. **There is no afterlife**. In many religions, the purpose of leading a good life is to ensure oneself a worthy afterlife. But

I happen to know for a fact that there is no afterlife. There are no pearly gates, there is no heaven, and there is certainly no God. There isn't even an angel like the one in Frank Capra's Christmas classic, *A Wonderful Life*, and that really broke my heart. But the good news is that there's no hell either. There are no devils with pitchforks, no everlasting brimstone stench, no pools of lava, no Faustian bargains to be made. There is not even an evil man who can rig the world series, like the devil in my favorite musical *Damn Yankees*. So it really doesn't matter how the hell you lead this life. So stop making an effort right now!

7. **Don't be good. Or bad.** Another nursery school myth is "Be a good girl," or "Be a good boy," and furthermore, "Bad boys and bad girls will be punished." When you accept sloth, you accept a world without punishment in either the next life, or even in this one. Karma's not a boomerang. If you find something nice that doesn't belong to you, but the Lost and Found is too much of a detour, don't worry. As a sloth, you have no obligation to turn it in. However, if returning that lost item is just the easier thing to do, go right ahead and do it. You can't get enough rewards for easy virtue.

8. **You are your own sloth.** In a Lockeian type of social contract, sloths are responsible for their own slothfulness. You can't rely on other people to be lazy for you. What if

they let you down and do some work on your behalf? With rights come responsibility, and you alone must ensure that you are a successful sloth. There is no sloth police, because policing is not in the sloth mentality.

9. **Sloth sex**. I am often asked about sex during the two-week induction period. Sex can destroy lethargiosis because it can be too exciting, even when you don't plan for it to be. Sex has a nasty habit of surprising you. However, after the two-week induction period, I suggest you concentrate on sex in which your partner does all the work. Everything you've ever read about needing to satisfy your partner sexually is wrong. They need to satisfy you. For the first time in your life, lie back and let them do it to you. I find, especially for my women patients, this is a revelatory experience. If you have trouble making this transition, I do make house calls. Please make sure to e-mail your picture to my website if my sexual services are something in which you may be interested.

10. **Nothing is urgent.** And I do mean nothing. For the first two weeks, I want you to remember there is absolutely no reason to get up for anything. Even an emergency. Believe me, someone else will take care of it, or it's not worth taking care of. If your house is burning down, your neighbors will put out the fire or their houses will burn down too. I want you to take a moment now and imagine the worst thing that

could possibly happen. Now pretend it's already happened. What can you do to stop it? We're all powerless ants in the grand scheme of the universe. Nothing we can do has any real effect anyway. God is dead. And if you don't believe me, read Nietzsche. But don't read him during the lethargiosis period.

Now lie back. You've begun! Sloth away! And remember, don't drink more than one glass of water per day.

CHAPTER SEVEN

Phase One: Getting Started

The Most Frequently Asked Questions During Lethargiosis

Now you are in the midst of the two-week lethargiosis period, and I know questions will inevitably come up. You are not sloth enough yet to realize that even asking a question requires too much energy. So I am happy to answer the most FAQs (Frequently Answered Questions).

1. **Can I be vertical?** No. At least, not during lethargiosis. Afterwards, I suggest a gradual reintroduction to vertical movement. Ultimately, a sloth can do whatever the hell he or she wants. But during this very important two-week period, you have to zap all activity from your body. We are victims of activity-based propaganda from the moment we enter society, and the point of lethargiosis is to purge your system of these lies.

2. **What can I read?** First of all, I would read this book over and over again. Let it be as frontlets between thine eyes. I would also like to suggest literature that will aid you in getting to sleep, including the children's classics *Goodnight Moon, Pat the Bunny, Goodnight, Elmo,* and *Clifford the Big Red Dog.* If you insist on reading novels, I suggest Thomas Pynchon's *Gravity's Rainbow* or Milton's epic poem *Paradise Lost* and its sequel, *Paradise Regained.* The plays of Samuel Beckett are also very restful, especially the appropriately titled *Endgame,* in which the characters live in garbage cans. I also recommend the unabridged Oxford English Dictionary, which you can revisit every time you need to snooze. The sloth song book (see website for details) offers a variety of ditties, which you can read and sing on your couch. One of my favorite songs is George Gershwin's immortal "I'm Biding My Time." I also like the lyrics "Counting flowers

on the wall, / that don't bother me at all / Smoking cigarettes and watching Captain Kangaroo, / Now don't tell me / I've nothin' to do."

3. **What should I wear?** I suggest loose-fitting clothing. I personally like light blue pajamas. Some of my patients prefer robes or T-shirts and sweatpants. Wear nothing that shows the shape of your body or is in anyway constricting. Pullovers also require less effort than zippers or buttons.

4. **Should I answer the phone?** If you have prepared for lethargiosis correctly, you shouldn't be receiving too many calls during this wonderful period. But should the phone ring, do not answer it. In fact, you may just want to take the phone off the hook before lying down. Once you emerge from lethargiosis successfully, you can chat on your phone

while lying down, as long as it's not an exertion. This means no conversations with in-laws or narcissistic mothers.

5. **Will I get bored?** You may at first, but you will begin to look at boredom as a very good thing. No one, not even two-year-olds, needs constant stimulation. The constant explosion of images and music on MTV and other teen channels is meant to alleviate boredom, but in reality it makes us addicted to constant stimulation. The state of boredom is devoid of anxiety, and is thus desirable to a sloth. Boredom has been given a negative spin, but in fact it is a desirable state. A successful sloth aspires to boredom.

6. **How will I meet anyone new?** In the first two weeks, you won't. But let me assure you, the sloth movement is a growing one. There are millions of American citizens who identify themselves as cybersloths. And, I am happy to say, there is also a growing movement of sloth in communist China.

7. **Will I get depressed?** No, because there's nothing to get depressed about. If you eliminate all competition from your life, all ambition, and all stress and pressure, you are free to be happy in an inert state.

8. **So what's the point of being alive?** Being alive is like getting a gift you didn't ask for. You could return it, but that's in poor taste and hurtful. So instead, you have to accept the

gift of living with as little resistance as possible. And for heaven's sakes, enjoy it. Getting a gift you don't want is better than not getting one at all.

If there are no more questions, let us proceed to phase two in your program.

CHAPTER EIGHT

Phase Two: In the Swing

Congratulations! You've gotten through lethargiosis. Now you're ready to be a full-time sloth. You've shocked your body into a comatose-like state for two weeks, and now I will give you a program you can live with more easily and still achieve slothdom. I like to call this program "Still Lowering Our Total Heart rate Too," or S L O T H Step Two.

Start by counting activity grams. For example, walking across a room is a standard, two-gram activity. Riding a stationary bike, on the other hand, is a four-hundred gram activity. Eating a chocolate bar is a five-gram activity. Thinking is a one-thousand gram activity. Stationary sex, on the other hand, is a three-gram activity. I will allow you fifty grams of activity a day. To help you get started, let's make a sample day's activity chart.

Sample Daily Activity Chart

- 10:30 A.M. Wake up   10 grams

- 11:15 A.M. Eat a Krispy Kreme donut
  and Sleepytime Tea   5 grams

- 11:30 A.M. Watch Cartoon Network   5 grams

- 12:30 P.M. Read the *New York Times*   30 grams

- 12:32 P.M. Put down the *New York Times*
  in exchange for *In Style* magazine,
  then read another article about
  Sarah Jessica Parker's favorite
  shoes she wore on *Sex in the City*

		In this case, *In Style* cancels out the *Times* activity grams and the total becomes	20 grams
•	1:00 P.M.	Order in lunch	3 grams
•	1:30 P.M.	Eat pepperoni pizza	15 grams
•	2:00 P.M.	Nap	Bonus negative 30 grams!
•	4:00 P.M.	Make phone call to stockbroker and discover your portfolio has increased 15 percent in its worth	10 grams
•	5:00 P.M.	Cocktail hour (drink straight vodka)	5 grams
•	6:15 P.M.	Conversation with a friend	10 grams
•	6:45 P.M.	A Cheeto dinner	8 grams
•	7:00 P.M.	Stationary sex	3 grams
•	7:10 P.M.	Sleep	0 grams

TOTAL: 64 grams of activity

So we went fourteen grams over our fifty-gram daily activity allotment. Whether or not you go over, don't stress. Remember, this is sloth. There is no sloth police, except for me. I suggest you look at this day again and visualize it better. What could you have cut out in order to save three grams? The obvious activity-guzzler is the *New York Times*. If you have to read the news, I suggest a tabloid paper with large print and color photos about celebrities. It's not a bad idea to read about famous sport stars, for instance, because it eliminates your own urge to play. For instance, none of us could ever be as talented as Michael Jordan or Tiger Woods, so why bother? The *New York Post*, for instance, which often features large stories about the New York Yankees, is useful for this kind of transference activity reduction.

All Systems No

I suggest, for once in your life, you make the right choices. Any revolutionary, from George Washington to Vladimir Lenin, has famously said that the key to change is seizing the means of production. But I am saying this in a new way. I want you to seize the means of production in your own life and shut them down. I want you to realize, probably for the first time in your life, that you have the right to be lazy. You can choose not to respond. You can choose not to move.

The Antidote

I want you to visualize—now, and anytime you get a craving for movement—the perfect sloth antidote to any activity. In other words, if you feel like running, remember, you could be sleeping. If you feel like participating, remember, you could be watching. If you feel like swimming, you could be floating. If you feel aggressive, you could be regressing. If you feel like climbing Mt. Everest, remember, you've got a 50-percent chance of falling off and dying. If you feel like creating, really think hard if you have the ability to create anything totally new.

Stay the Course!

I want you to visualize what truly makes you happy. Aren't you always happiest at the end of the day, when your work is done, the children are in bed, everyone is fed, and it's time to veg out? What I am offering you is a permanent state of vegetation, without being a vegetable. I want you to visualize a life without worries or cares, a life without pride or obligations. If you practice these visualization exercises every day, I personally promise that you will remain on the path to slothdom.

Now I know some of you are saying I'm being hypocritical. Here I am, asking you to "practice." Aren't I philosophically opposed to practicing? I want to make this very clear. What I'm asking you to practice is not making any efforts at all. Our school systems are polluted with aphorisms like, "It doesn't matter if you win or lose; it's how you play the game," and "Pride in Performance." In order to erase those from your mind-set, it will take some energy. But remember, you can get energy deductions by reading *In Style* magazine or spending a day watching the Weather Channel.

Clutter Your Mind with Nonsense

Finally, once you have managed to learn to involuntarily count activity grams, I would like you to really focus on cluttering your mind with nonsense. In other words, if what you think about is, "Who is the reality-TV bachelor going to marry" or "Are Monica Lewinsky's handbags really selling," you'll find that it's really not worth thinking at all. For instance, during one of my brush-up sloth periods, I deliberately watched reruns of Joan Rivers and her daughter Melissa interviewing nominees for the Golden Globe awards about their respective gowns. As Joan gushed to Nicole Kidman about her Chanel dress, I thought to myself, "Why am I bothering with this?" Then Joan moved on to Jennifer Lopez and asked to see her engagement ring. I followed the story of her on-again-off-again engagement for the next two years, and realized that whether I liked it or not, I was being forced to know more about this woman than I ever wanted or needed to. I began to look at most things in my life that way, and it became easier to eliminate them. The more you clutter your mind, the more you realize there is no reason to intake most of the nonsense that is put in front of us.

CHAPTER NINE

Plateaus

Now comes the question that everyone asks me at this juncture. I get at least one thousand hits on my website regarding this one issue. What if I plateau? What if I don't feel myself losing energy? What if my body reaches a stasis?

This is difficult with sloth, because plateau is, in a way, what we are aspiring to. But I don't want you to stop too soon. I don't want you to give up. Because as long as there's still just a little energy in your body, you will still think, "Maybe I can cheat. Maybe I can go to the gym. Maybe I can get an A. Maybe I could get a little more money than my neighbor. Maybe I could clean up my room. Maybe I could even—and I hate to say the word— diet."

(Don't) Get Sloppy!

My answer to those of you who feel stuck is that you've gotten sloppy. You're not being meticulous enough in your activity counting. You're not using your visualization techniques, and I suspect you are not using any of my sloth products.

Stock up!

In addition to the sloth songbook, there are many other sloth products that can get you past your plateau. May I suggest, first, my sloth breakfast bars. Packed with sugar, additives, and a delicious touch of Ambien sleeping tablets, the breakfast bar is bound to lead you into an induced slothlike state. Or, for those of you who prefer a powdered drink, you might consider my "Breakfast of Non-Champions Milkshake." I especially like to recommend these shakes to those of you who have been avoiding dairy. My secret recipe is to add in double-chocolate-chip Haagen Daz ice cream swirled with Ben & Jerry's Heath Bar Crunch. Believe you me, it's the kind of breakfast that will take your get-up-and-go and make it got-up-and-gone.

For daytime distraction may I also suggest my special Silly Putty balls. Do you remember Silly Putty from when we were young? The chewing-gum-like substance that you could pull and pull and pull? I have found, for those who have plateaued and feel they need something to concentrate on, pulling Silly Putty really helps.

Another way to accelerate the sloth process is focusing on impossible present-day political quagmires. Remember, I don't want you to look for solutions but rather to feel defeated and enervated by mess. I have also published my own evaluation of Middle East politics. In this surface examination, you will see there is absolutely no answer to this multifaceted situation.

Speaking of the Middle East, I have just introduced a tobacco line into my roster of products. Do you remember when everyone had a cigarette after sex because it was relaxing? Well, now that we're all so busy talking about the cancerous effects of smoking cigarettes, we have forgotten its pleasures. For those who have plateaued in sloth, I suggest smoking, and of course leaving the ashes and butts all over the floor. Smoking really reminds us how pleasant an unfastidious life can be.

And don't forget about my plateau beauty products. I have just introduced a line of more than a hundred colors of nail polish. While you're slothing, it might be enjoyable to paint your toes as the day's activity. Nail painting fits perfectly into the sloth's regimen because it requires almost no energy expenditure, and it renders your hands or feet inoperable while the polish is drying.

Also may I suggest my full line of facial masks, some of which need to be left on for seven days. For instance, my Dead Sea moisturizing mask, which will exfoliate your skin back to when you were still in the womb, takes two days to apply and five days to congeal. I also have hand cream, body cream, and lip mustache remover. In addition, I am planning to introduce this fall an entire line of hair products. While slothing, there's no harm in enriching your highlights with long-lasting deep color, revitalizing your roots, and increasing your hair's body and shine.

Cybersloth games can also aid in plateaus. I have developed two thousand solitaire variations, and an equal amount of Tetris games to keep you occupied during the most trying of times. Finally, the true sloth can enter a virtual sloth reality, where your character must spend as much time on a cybercouch as possible. Your virtual sloth, like your actual self, must avoid the temptation of interaction and activity at all costs. Every year, the highest scorer of Virtual Sloth is sent a new hammock by my company.

And finally, in times of plateau, I really want you to consider having stationary sex. If you don't want me to come over and have it with you, you can find (on my website) volunteers who will let you lie there and take it. I really have no prejudices against straight or gay sex, as long as you don't actively participate. But I have found that a little sloth sex gets the juices flowing just enough without interfering in the sloth regimen.

WARNING: Do not fall in love!

Do not get involved! Do not put yourself in any kind of relationship you have to work at. If the relationship doesn't work by itself, without any investment from either partner, it's not worth keeping.

Once you have passed your plateau, you are ready to move on to sloth maintenance. Here we go!

CHAPTER TEN

Maintaining Your Sloth

I want you to ask yourself honestly, "Have I really won the battle against activity? Do I really prefer to disengage than get involved? Is there anything that still makes me feel stress?" At this juncture, you should be stress and anxiety free.

Prepare for Permanent Sloth

Because you have been in a state of sloth for some months now, you have already created a routine to help you stay slothful for the rest of your life. I hope you have eliminated all those triggers in your life that make you feel guilty. For instance, I hope you have rid your house of any alumnae magazine that reminds you your school chums are still out there achieving. By now I hope you have rid your life of anyone you could possibly be genuinely attracted to. Remember that true love often can cause passion, and passion is the biggest enemy of sloth. Passion inevitably leads to bitterness. And sloths are a contented lot.

Now that you are in maintenance, you can increase your grams of activity from fifty to seventy-five. For instance, if you want to play the ukulele while lying down, knock yourself out. Masturbation, which is not permitted during lethargiosis, or during initial slothdom, is absolutely okay during maintenance. And you might want to send away for a few of my magazines, which are designed to get you just aroused enough so that masturbation is enjoyable, but not overwhelming. Be careful of traditional pornography, which does not walk this fine line.

In the maintenance phase, feel free to watch any of Julia Roberts's movies, which are entertaining but not challenging. I personally avoid her movie with Hugh Grant because Hugh Grant gets me too excited. Another favorite entertainment of mine during maintenance is a series of documentaries I produced titled *The Great Thinkers*. Each of these movies is a six-hour, in-depth tribute to the most influential minds in civilization. I start with Archimedes, then do a special twelve-hour on our old friend St. Thomas Aquinas. I make a compelling case that the sadness, which Aquinas thought alienated monks from their duty to God, was actually what kept them from going mad and talking to the animals like Francis of Assisi.

If Duty Calls

Samantha Burkowski of Oakwood Apartments, Glen Ridge, California, wrote me a question I always share at this point with my maintenance patients. Samantha asks, "What can I do to prevent reengagement with activity? How can I stop the temptation to move?" What I told Samantha, and I have to tell you, is that addiction is a very tricky thing. We are all addicted to pleasing others. Since we were tiny tots, our parents have told us to be good girls and boys, to do our homework, and to grow up and be successful. It is almost impossible not to be tempted back into proving ourselves. Like any other addiction, you must overcome your need to do anything—one day at a time. Thinking about a full work-free life might overwhelm you. My answer is to just try to do nothing one day at a time. Make a real effort not to put anything away one day at a time. Every day, try not to live up to anyone's expectations, even your own. With the help of Samantha, I have started sloth chat rooms that you can access from the safety of your couch. These chat rooms provide all of the support and encouragement that accompany traditional support groups but without the inconvenience of having to leave your home.

If you find yourself getting into real trouble, put yourself back on the stringent lethargiosis program. Everybody wants to cheat now and then. But if you find yourself making five consecutive business calls, or doing a few crunches when you think no one's looking, I beg of you, go back on strict lethargiosis. Lethargiosis is a reset button when your life schedule gets out of hand. And remember, there will be those who will try to lure you back into activity: your parents, your lovers, your boss, your accountant, the IRS. When their pressure becomes too much, and you think you're breaking down, pick up this book, or call me, and I will talk you through it and get you back to lethargiosis.

Remember, You Did It!

Remember, being a sloth should give you a sense of confidence that will spill over into the rest of your life. You have finally taken control of your life, in the way you have always wished you could.

You've done more than just drop out—you've permanently removed yourself from the brainwashed arena that is twenty-first-century life. Chances are, you won't think another original thought. But in many ways, no one really wants you to. You can take real pride that you have bucked the trend. You finally don't need to come up with a reason not to go to every party that's being thrown. And, you can happily fire all your household staff.

Remember the "Too Much Ten"

Here's a list of ten people that history regards as winners and whom I regard as losers. They are dangerous role models. Their anti-sloth stories, by example, contribute to the sanity of investing in the maintenance of a lifetime of sloth.

1. **William the Conqueror:** The bastard son who won the Battle of Hastings in 1066. William was born a bastard, which is a birthright to slothenliness. But he felt a need to overcompensate. By bringing the Normans to England he became responsible for the proliferation of the crossbow. Wouldn't he have been better off having bastard children of his own in France?

2. **Marie Curie:** The great scientist and female role model. Although Madame Curie was the first woman ever to win a Nobel Prize, and the first person to win two, her continued exposure to radioactive material through her work led to her own death. If she had laid off the research and the Nobel Prizes, she would've led a longer and happier life.

3. **Lord Byron:** Famous nineteenth-century romantic poet. Born with a clubfoot, Lord Byron had the perfect excuse to lounge on a chaise for his entire life. He could've written volumes and volumes of poetry while resting. (In sloth maintenance, you are allowed to write poems.) Instead, he fled England to escape scandal and died of a fever while fighting in the Greek War of Independence in 1824.

4. **Leon Trotsky:** Russian Revolutionary. Trotsky was killed by a deranged anticommunist with an ice pick in Mexico. Look at Russia now.

5. **William Shakespeare:** Playwright, etc. Shakespeare wrote so many plays that we don't really know if he actually wrote them all. Perhaps if he had rested a little bit more, there'd be less chitchat about Christopher Marlowe.

6. **Eli Whitney:** Cotton gin inventor. Although inventions that encourage mass production feel pro-sloth, they in fact increase expectations of overall productivity in a profoundly anti-sloth way. The cotton gin encouraged slavery, and sloth is defiantly antislavery. I'm not interested in people finding other people to do work for them—I'm interested in not doing work at all.

7. **Jack LaLanne:** American exercise guru, who made people think they had to get in shape. Through his example, he made it possible for Arnold Schwarzenegger to ultimately become the governor of California.

8. **Mother Theresa:** Now a saint, she dedicated her life to working for an improved quality of life for the poor in third-world countries. I have nothing against feeding the hungry— sloths are not interested in starvation. In fact, I'm all for feeding the hungry. But I am against good work being intricately related to God, since embracing God is the anti-

sloth. The only thing you should be embracing is your blanket.

9. **Paul Newman:** Hollywood actor, American icon, and entrepreneur. You might be surprised to find a Hollywood actor on this list. But Paul Newman, in addition to being a great actor, is also a race-car driver, a Democratic party activist, and a food entrepreneur. I am not opposed to eating Newman's popcorn on the couch while watching one of his movies, particularly *Cat on a Hot Tin Roof* because he looks so fetching in that undershirt. But the story of his life inspires other actors to entrepreneurship, owning restaurants, and developing political interest. Actors should memorize their lines and go home.

10. **My Mother:** My mother raised nine children by herself. She cooked. She cleaned. She loved my father. She danced as a principal in the New York City Ballet and was also a principal of a public high school in the Bronx. She was a volunteer at Mt. Sinai hospital, and every Christmas, after she had attended to all of her familial responsibilities, she left to work in a soup kitchen. She had two lovers (a judge and a garbage man), and she also fed us organic food. No one will ever be as great a mother as she, and in that way, she really let me down.

Memorize this list. Anytime you feel like going back to work, remember how their celebrated achievements undermined their lives and society at large.

In the next chapter, however, I will present you with breaking news about the health benefits of sloth from a joint study from the Rockefeller Institute and Kraft Cheese.

CHAPTER ELEVEN

Medical Breakthrough: Sloth Is the Way to Good Health!

At a recent women's health luncheon in New York, Jane Brody, the personal health editor for the *New York Times*, reported, "We all have stress in our lives, between work, families and juggling busy schedules. . . . The trick is to avoid long-term stress, which can contribute to serious health problems, such as high blood pressure, obesity and diabetes. . . . Stress can play a major role in our immune system's ability to maintain a healthy equilibrium, possibly making us more susceptible to illness."

Cases in Pointlessness

The following findings are based on a five-year study whereby ten individuals were followed through scenarios of varying stress levels. The results are shocking. Although these are extreme stress scenarios, they will give you some indication of what can happen if you don't choose sloth.

Case #1. Helen Yaeger of Muncie, Indiana. Helen Yaeger's mother was dying of Alzheimer's. She had two children in nursery school, and a third child who was blind, deaf, and dumb. Her husband lost both of his hands in a reaper accident on his farm, which was subsequently repossessed by the U.S. government. Helen, who was a religious woman, thought if she believed in God she could handle it all. One day Helen's mother ran naked through the town of Muncie, while Helen's children accidentally drank turpentine instead of milk at lunch. Her disabled child started an electric fire in her home, which caused the house to burn down, and her unemployed husband tried to seduce their next-door neighbor with his feet. The overwhelming stress, which Helen always thought she could deal with because of her strong faith in God, caused her blood pressure to spontaneously rise to 400/300. She went to church to pray, passed out while kneeling, and hit her head on a pew. She was rushed to the hospital and slipped into a coma from which she has yet to emerge. Helen is a prime example of how stress can destroy you. If only she had put her mother in a state home, abandoned her blind child, killed her husband, and sent her remaining two children to become Gap models, she could've sold the farm and rested in a hammock.

Case #2. Jeremy Strong of New Canaan, Connecticut. Jeremy always dreamed of public office. He wanted to serve. He was a man who fed on the excitement of public life. Jeremy wanted to be everywhere, with all of the right, powerful people, making important decisions all of the time. His whole life was spent achieving this goal—he majored in government at Oberlin, and was a Rhodes Scholar at Oxford. Ever since first grade he was his class president, and in graduate school he became the first American student body president at Oxford University. When Jeremy returned to his home state of Connecticut, he ran for public office. Having successfully served two terms as his state's governor, he was considering running for president. On the night he was to announce his bid for the presidency, political rivals sabotaged him. They fabricated evidence that Jeremy had been embezzling money from the state of Connecticut to pay for the gold sinks in each bathroom of his house. They also leaked a video tape to the *National Enquirer* showing his wife sleeping with their nanny, a nineteen-year-old former Junior Miss Connecticut. On the same day, Jeremy was forced to deal with terrorism threats in all the Coach Leather Goods Stores in Connecticut, and twenty tabs of Ecstasy were planted in what he thought was his multiple vitamin. Disgraced, humiliated, and broken, Jeremy was forced to withdraw from the presidential race; he became a joke on all the late-night talk shows. Inspired by the scandal, his wife and nanny did actually run off together. Having hit rock bottom, Jeremy took all twenty of those Ecstasy tabs and was photographed humping the staircase at the Westport train station. Although it was eventually revealed that all of the charges against him had been trumped up, the damage was done. Jeremy can still be found with that staircase, where we suspect he will live out his days. Had Jeremy had no aspirations, he wouldn't have built a life so easily destroyed by a few errant rumors to the press.

Case #3. Sara Salzberger of Tampa, Florida. Sara Salzberger was a Boca Raton aerobics instructor who had dreams of becoming a reality television star. She wanted to be the next Joe Millionaire. Her diligent efforts, however, only resulted in being picked up for *Survivor 47: The Nile.* During the second group challenge, a three-legged race, Sara attempted to take a shortcut that resulted in her galloping through a nest of deeply poisonous asps. She was bitten and landed in a hospital that was under attack by fundamentalist Muslims. The confusion caused by the attack led the doctors to accidentally amputate her leg; during her recovery Sara was mistaken for an heiress and kidnapped by the attacking fundamentalists. Her kidnappers are still holding her in a cave, until they receive $100 million from the Boca Raton Reserve. If Sara had been content as a Florida aerobics instructor, she would happily be leading a step class today.

Case #4. Tiffany Trento of Los Angeles, California. Tiffany was an aspiring actress in Los Angeles and always trying to better herself. Her days were scheduled with hair appointments, skin appointments, exercise appointments, elocution appointments, and stylist appointments. She waitressed all night at a Denny's hamburger joint to pay for them. Intimidated by her competition, Tiffany decided she had to alter her appearance. She got Botox in her face, Liptox in her lips, she had an eye job, a nose job, a face-lift, liposuction, and reduced the length of her second toe by half an inch so she could fit into pointy high-heeled shoes. By the time she was finished remaking herself, Tiffany bore more resemblance to a Siamese cat than the young ingénue roles for which she was being sent out. Finally, she got a call from a producer whom she often served at Denny's, who wanted to give her a break. But when she arrived at the audition, she was unrecognizable and didn't get the part. Convinced that she lost the part because was still not thin enough, she decided to have two ribs removed. Complications during surgery arose, and her entire rib cage was accidentally removed. She is now a human Gumby, and although her career has flourished as an animated cartoon, she has great difficulty breathing, swallowing, walking, talking, and sitting straight. Wouldn't Tiffany have been better off accepting her God-given features, and even putting on a little weight? Narcissism is the anti-sloth, and should be avoided at all costs.

Case #5. Timothy Godwin of Kingston, Jamaica. Timothy was the ninth of eleven children. His mother was a laundress at the Kingston Marriott, and he had no idea who his father was. Timothy wanted to better himself. One day he swam from Montego Bay all the way to Naples, Florida. When he arrived, he became a cabana boy at the Ritz Carlton Hotel, where he befriended a niece of the Rockefeller family, who was on spring break from Vassar College. Timothy fell in love immediately and decided to do anything to be in her league. He began by holding up the local Wendy's restaurant with great ease. After that, he went on a fast-food holdup spree, including Burger

King, McDonald's, Popeye's Chicken, Taco Bell, Teriyaki Boy, Pizza Hut, and Arby's. He then went to Ralph Lauren and bought himself a new wardrobe. When he wasn't burglarizing, Timothy was taking high school equivalency (GED) courses and studying for the SATs. Timothy was accepted on full scholarship to Vassar. But two weeks into his freshman year, he held up Juliet's Brick Oven Pizzeria across the street from the Vassar campus for a little extra cash. On the night he produced a diamond engagement ring for Miss Rockefeller, the state police arrived. In short order, he was recognized as the Florida fast-food burglar and sentenced to jail for twenty-five years to life. When he was cuffed and taken away, Miss Rockefeller looked at him and said, "How could you? This story isn't even as good as Theodore Dreiser's *An American Tragedy*." Mr. Godwin should've stayed in Jamaica, smoking ganja and letting his mother support him instead of coming to this country and thinking he could get a great education and marry up.

Case #6. Renee Molanphy of Minneapolis, Minnesota. Renee believed she could change the world through political activism. When she was in college, she joined peace marches, she organized the local soup kitchen staff, she picketed for better faculty wages, she refused to touch any paper that wasn't environmentally sound, she wrote petitions for the release of political prisoners, she marched on Washington every chance she could get, she worked in an abortion clinic, she performed gay marriages in her college dorm room, and she helped register voters in underprivileged areas of Minneapolis. Renee sent care packages to the civilians in Kosovo and Iraq who had survived the wars, and she sent all her savings to political causes. One morning at 2 A.M., when Renee was home after a "Take Back the Night" rally, there was a knock on her door. She was confronted by FBI and Her Majesty's Secret Service officers, who accused her of being a Communist Muslim Environmentalist Pro-Choice Anarchistic, and among the ten most dangerous women in the United States and Great Britain. She was sent immediately to Guantanamo Bay for questioning and hasn't been heard from since. If Renee had focused more on her own happiness as opposed to the happiness of others, she could be married and living in Minneapolis right now.

Case #7. Roy Goldberg of Rockville Center, Long Island. When Roy Goldberg was growing up, he couldn't keep his hands off his sister's Barbie dolls. He loved to make them sing and dance to all his favorite Barbra Streisand and Judy Garland records. By the time Roy was twelve, his favorite activity was combing his mother's hair and trying on her mink coat. When Roy was a senior in high school, he fell in love with Johnny

Akron, the captain of his high-school varsity football team. The night Roy told Johnny how much he loved him, Johnny gave him a black eye. From that night on, Roy vowed that he would not accept a life in the closet, and would do everything he could to ensure that he and others could live their lives openly. Roy became a very successful Broadway general manager; he even got to escort Carol Channing to the Tony Awards. Roy met his partner, Mel, at a Broadway Bares Benefit, and they were together for ten years. Then, last month at the theater, Dick Cheney, the vice president of the United States, arrived to tell Roy he had to get married. Roy said, "That's great—Mel and I have been meaning to get married for years!" The veep said, "No, no, you have to marry a woman, and I brought one with me. I'd like you to meet Judy Shapiro. She's very depressed and hardly talks, but I'm sure she'll snap out of it after the wedding." Roy broke down into tears. "Why aren't I guaranteed the rights to life, liberty, and the pursuit of happiness, like every other American citizen?" Dick Cheney looked at him and said, "Because you're not like every other American citizen. You're a fruitcake." Roy and Judy were married at Bellevue hospital, where they've been ever since—in the mental care unit. If only Roy had been slothful about revealing his sexuality, he could've lived a long and happy life, and continued his secret, unacknowledged/unlegitimized life with Mel.

Case #8. Hattie Bjornson of Omaha, Nebraska. Hattie prided herself on her housekeeping. As she raised her children, she would tell them, "You know, children, the deadliest sin of them all is sloth." If her children were too lazy to clean their room or put their toys away, she would say, "I don't want you acting like that animal that hangs upside down and sucks on leaves all day." Hattie had the cleanest house in Omaha. You could lick her kitchen floors. Every year she won the Omaha Lady's Auxiliary Award for Best Housekeeping. Hattie was also penny-wise, and told her children to always save everything for a rainy day. Hattie had all her receipts in different boxes: one for dinners, one for clothing, one for movies, one for all her children's school supplies. And then one day, Hattie won the Publisher's Clearing House Sweepstakes, from which she had been saving all her receipts for the past forty years. As the grand prize winner, she was FedExed a check for $100 million immediately. Hattie was so excited she hid the check in a special safe place. Her husband urged her to deposit the check immediately, but she said, "No, no. I'm Hattie Bjornson. I know where everything is." That night, her husband took her out to celebrate. During dinner, the strain of being so neat for the past forty years plus the excitement of winning, proved too much for Hattie. She had a brain aneurysm, which resulted in amnesia. She could not remember where she had put the $100 million check. Her husband and children emptied out every drawer. The house became a mess. Hattie, looking at her house in complete disarray, had a second, more dangerous aneurysm and has not recovered to this day, nor has her family found the well-hidden check. If Hattie had only been a lousy housekeeper and spent all of her money, none of this would've happened.

Case #9. Real Chen of San Francisco, California. Real Chen was really healthy. He checked every label of every food he ever ate to make sure there were no additives. He never smoked, he never drank, he never stayed out past 9 P.M., he walked every day for four miles in the morning, he swam every day in the evening, he never ate sugar, he never ate dairy, he never ate wheat, he never ate fat, and he only ate organic foods. He never spent more than thirty minutes in the sun without sun block, he washed his hands before, after, and during every meal, he wiped off surfaces in other people's houses, he wore a mask on airplanes and in the subway, he made anyone he had sex with wear a latex bodysuit, and he never shook hands without wearing gloves. At his favorite organic co-op, Real began scooping pumpkin granola into his bag. Unbeknownst to him, a true sadist had just poured anthrax spores into that granola bin, thinking that getting the healthiest first would make his point more dramatically. The sadist believed in a kind of

inverted Darwinism in which only the least fit should survive. Real became the first and only casualty in this short-lived bacteria war. If only Real had stayed home on his couch and ordered in Dominos Pizza, he would be alive today.

Case #10. Michael Barakiva of Twin Rivers, New Jersey. Michael's Armenian, Israeli, Cambodian, and Bosnian heritage made him the only quadruple genocide descendant in central New Jersey. Michael was a sloth until the famous Princeton/Trenton war, in which Princeton attempted to become the first corporate university city-state. Michael was torn—his Cambodian and Armenian genes sided with Princeton, while his Israeli and Bosnian sides favored Trenton's position. Michael, who in high school was happy to stay home watching *Buffy the Vampire Slayer*, was suddenly energized. He fought for both sides, dedicated his efforts to Princeton in the first half of the week and Trenton in the latter. When he was exposed as a double agent, both sides joined and sought him out as a war criminal. His death was considered the only justifiable case of ethnic cleansing in the history of New Jersey. Ironically, his death also served to end the Trenton/Princeton conflict, and Princeton was happy to resume its place as the jewel of the Garden State. If only Michael had stayed true to his initial sloth impulses instead of defending his heritages, he'd be watching the Buffy season-three finale for the ninety-seventh time in the comfort of his suburban attached house basement.

To summarize, all of these scenarios present cases in which a slothful attitude would've saved the lives of the various studies. For further details on any of these individuals, go to www.sloth.com, and click on "Extreme Challenge."

In the next chapter, I have exciting news about the new twenty-first-century sloths. They may not look like one of us, but they achieve slothdom in a subtle and camouflaging way. So, in this very latest addition of *Sloth: And How to Get It*, I had to include a chapter on the übersloth.

CHAPTER TWELVE

A Pause in the Proceeding

I am suddenly overcome with exhaustion. I know it's time to write to you about the twenty-first-century movement of übersloths, but I just can't do it right now. I have been working on this book for thirty years and napping after each paragraph. I have developed carpal tunnel syndrome while writing it, and the fire department has been at my house twenty times because of mold and the stench emanating from it.

As you can well guess, I am a dedicated sloth. I practice what I preach. I don't feel I should even finish this book. But, I am such a firm believer in the sloth lifestyle that, against my better judgment, I am willing to make the smallest of efforts to complete this work. Excuse me, while I take another nap, having just finished another paragraph.

Z Z Z Z Z Z Z Z Z Z Z Z Z Z Z Z Z Z Z Z Z Z Z Z Z Z Z Z Z Z Z Z Z Z Z Z Z Z Z

Rest

Well, that was refreshing. I can't stress enough—and know that I only use this word advisedly—how much sloth changed my life. In my time, I practiced all the seven deadly sins. And the only cure I had from being a lustful, avaricious, envious, gluttonous, proud, angry man was to commit myself to sloth. Sloth purged my body of all my sinful urges and brought me into a new consciousness, which I like to call "The New Apathy."

Who Cares?

First, let me share with you a little trick I use when there is more work to do and I just don't feel like doing it. I shut my eyes, I go to sleep, and I play Muzak on my computer. I am particularly fond of the Muzak version of "Raindrops Keep Falling On My Head," and "The Pachelbel Canon." I empty my mind of all thoughts and deadlines, and imagine that I'm floating on a raft with nowhere to go. When I wake up and see my papers all over the room, and yesterday's lunch, and last month's pizza crust, I feel that I am finally in a place where I make up my own rules, and my motivations are pure. From this place, I can approach the work again without caring about it. And that lack of care is what has made this book, in its first edition, a worldwide best-seller. I have never appeared on any talk show unless the crew was willing to come to my house to interview me. I sign books only while resting in a hammock, and all the quotes that were obtained for this book jacket came to me through e-mail. Unlike any other lifestyle or diet book you will ever read, this one was completely written on my back. My idea of a book tour consists of writing one chapter in the bedroom and the other in my backyard.

It's Your Fault, Not Mine

Excuse me, I'm getting so tired writing this now that I have to take another rest before I finish. And by the way, if this book doesn't make much sense, it's your fault, not mine. Your mind is still rigidly controlled and far too orderly. You need to enter a slothlike mental state to really appreciate this book.

Remember, if you are still trying to change your life, you haven't embraced sloth, and you will always be searching for something better. This is the best it's going to get. Don't look farther. Good night.

CHAPTER THIRTEEN

Überslothdom

In this, the last chapter, I have exciting news about the new twenty-first-century sloths. They may not look like one of us, but they achieve slothdom in a subtle and camouflaging way. So in this very latest addition of *Sloth: And How to Get It*, I am proud to present a chapter on the übersloths: the new breed of sloths.

Have you ever been lying on your couch, watching four well-groomed women of diverse ethnicities on television chatting about how they manage to get everything done? They call themselves "jugglers," and they're all able to have husbands, children, careers, social causes, plus they exercise three hours a day, eat only vegetables, and employ personal stylists to tell them what to wear every morning. Or, have you ever seen a man on television talking about how he made $100 million before he was thirty, then walked from New York to China, directed three Oscar-winning movies, got married four times, each time with better and better sex with a different gendered partner? In their outside façade, they are the anti-sloths—the doers and shakers. But just like in politics, where the extreme right and the extreme left meet, so in sloth the extremes merge into one another.

Now I know you're lying down eating a Milky Way with garbage surrounding you and thinking that now I've lost my mind. Any woman who is obsessed with her Palm Pilot, her Blackberry, and her cell phone can't possibly be construed as one of us. But here is what I think is the exciting news of the twenty-first century, and what I've been waiting to tell you in this latest addition. These übermotivated, overscheduled people are the new sloths. I hear you screaming from your couches, "This can't be true!" But now, I will tell you why.

When you achieve true slothdom, you have no desire for the world to change. True sloths are not revolutionaries. There is no possible dialectic. It doesn't matter if the world evolves, because your purpose is not to get things done. Sloths are neither angry nor hopeful. They are not even anarchists. Anarchy takes too much work. Sloths are the lazy guardians at the gate of the status quo.

So you may look at these overachievers and think to yourself, "Christ, they make me tired! And I certainly don't have anything in common with them. When they're doing Pilates at 7 A.M., I'm sleeping. When they're going to work, I'm still sleeping. And during their power lunch meetings, I'm probably taking a nap. Their switch is on, and mine is off."

I know some of you think I sound like a hypocrite here. I know what I've said about overachievers before. But this is the new revised edition. I've just come to these conclusions, so try to look at it from my perspective. Are these hyperscheduled, overactive individuals really creating anything new? Are they guilty of passion in any way? Do they have a new vision for their government? For their community? Or for themselves?

Their purpose is to keep themselves so busy, so entrenched in their active lives, that their spirit reaches a permanent state of lethargiosis. In other words, their hyperactivity is no different than your or my slothfulness. Whether you're a traditional sloth or a New Age übersloth, we are all looking at the possibility of real thought, and rejecting it. Better to fall into line then to question the going ethos, whether it be fashion, family, or even religion.

True creativity requires some amount of not just initiative but the courage to fall out of line. The new übersloths are always in step. They are eager not to shake the foundations of their position in society: their wealth, their power, and the privilege of their lives. The übersloth can spend an hour on a stationary bicycle in a spin class racing at 70 mph to nowhere. It is a metaphor for their lives, which are full of sound and fury, but like the best of sloths, signify nothing.

I don't want to be brag, but I would say that this twenty-first-century obsession with celebrity is part of the triumph of the new sloth lifestyle (I like to think of it as sloth lite). These celebrities seem to be very busy wearing Valentino designer wear, having babies, falling in love, appearing in romantic comedies, and probably achieving very little except for giving us all someone to read about and pleasantly filling the void. We know that none of them will really change the foundations of our times, since they all have a great stake in preserving their own status. Some celebrities do become involved in left-wing or right-wing politics, but when push comes to shove, they will not relinquish their celebrity status for their beliefs.

Like any organism, sloth evolves to survive in its environment. So this new breed of sloth is bringing our ennui into the twenty-first century. For myself, stylistically, I prefer to remain on my couch. But the creative, spiritual, and political void of these new übersloths makes me proud. Again, I want you to understand that previously I looked at these people and felt disgust, as I described in my first chapter about the aerobics instructor in the white bikini in Hawaii. But just as two-toed and three-toed sloths peacefully cohabit the same jungle, I watch these übersloth brethren with a sense of pride.

This doesn't mean in any way, that you, my loyal followers, who have come to a sense of traditional sloth through lethargiosis, should change anything. Sloths, as you know, are not comparative, and they are not competitive. I am certainly not asking you to evolve into the new übersloths. What I want you to see is that our combined numbers are larger than you think. In fact, sloths may be the largest growing global-interest group. Consider the advances in technology of laptops, microwaves, plasma televisions, and cell phones. These are all aimed for our convenience.

So, my dear friends and followers, we are coming to the end of this journey, which means you can turn over and rest, if you haven't taken a few naps already. By reading this book, you have embraced sloth as the most viable of the deadly sins. With sloth, you will live a longer, happier, and more rewarding life. You will release yourself from any expectations, false hope, or motivation. Unlike any other lifestyle, diet, or self-help manual now on the market, sloth—once achieved— takes very little to maintain. As I have told you, sloth will release you from all the terrible *shoulds* dominating your life. It will eliminate the nagging tug of passion, creativity, and individual drive. For once in your life, you will be

truly comfortable and anxiety free. And personal comfort is *much* more important than any achievement or social contract.

For those of you who are still not convinced by the growing sloth movement, who still believe the negative rap that sloth has gotten over the centuries and in the idiotic notion that sloth keeps you away from God, may I say you are probably all suffering from hypertension, ulcers, false hopes, romantic illusions, and communist leanings. Anyone who still truly believes in possibilities, whether political or personal, is delusional. If you have not embraced this book, or the sloth lifestyle, you are still living not only with hope but with a true belief in human potential. And if history has taught us nothing else, it has taught us that humans have yet to create a truly peaceful, loving world. Civil rights may come and go, great art may come and go, even religious saviors may come and go, but the limitations of a human life remain. Therefore, isn't it time now, at the beginning of the twenty-first century, to honestly embrace sloth before some fundamental righteousness gets us all blown up? Sloth won't create great civilizations, but it won't destroy them either. Isn't it time we kicked off our shoes, sat back, and said, "I give up."

In the following appendix, I will present you a new activity gram counter. There will also be a sloth network on channel 823, providing programming guaranteed not to stimulate or challenge in any way. It may be difficult to distinguish between this and other channels, but only on channel 823 can you watch me sleeping. I want to wish you all good luck and congratulate you on embarking on this important turn in your life. For many of you, I know it's been a long journey before you came to me. You will make some sacrifices in accepting sloth, but the rewards, believe me, will be greater. And remember, getting through this book is the last difficult thing you will ever have to do. The rest is going to be easy. The challenge is over. It's all downhill from here. And nothing *really* matters. Good luck. If I could, I would say I love you, but that takes too much effort. Sleep well, fellow sloths.

Appendix

Activity Gram Counter

Use this counter to gauge your daily activity. Remember, the recommended grams-per-day total is fifty until you hit maintenance, when you can increase to seventy-five. Many activities are entirely forbidden. For instance, if you really need to run, you can't move for the two weeks following to compensate for the activity gram expenditure. Please also note that certain activities are especially slothful and can actually eliminate your activity gram total for the day. These are listed as Negative Gram activities, and I especially encourage you to partake in them.

Eating and Drinking

Krispy Kreme donut and Sleepytime tea	5 grams
Order in lunch	3 grams
Pepperoni pizza	15 grams
Straight vodka	5 grams
A Cheeto dinner	8 grams
Chicken Caesar salad	30 grams
Sushi	20 grams
Twizzlers	2 grams
Anything you have to prepare at home	Triple normal gram value
Grilled fish	40 grams

Recreational

Watch Cartoon Network	5 grams
Watch CNN	50 grams
Conversation with a friend	10 grams
Conversation with a parent	100 grams
Bicycle riding	100 grams
Treadmill	200 grams
Running	500 grams
Rollerblading	1000 grams
Snowboarding	This is the wrong book for you
Virtual snowboarding	10 grams
Shopping	25 grams
Shopping online	10 grams

Reading

New York Times (uh oh!)	30 grams
This book	2 grams
Celebrity gossip magazine	5 grams
In Style magazine	3 grams
People magazine	Negative 5 grams
Catalogs	Negative 10 grams
Great turn-of-the-century Russian novels	100 grams
Any other self-help book	300 grams
The plays of William Shakespeare	400 grams

Love, Sex, and Romance

Kissing	50 grams
Stationary sex	3 grams
Active sex	200 grams

Masturbatory sex	100 grams
Getting married (heterosexual)	500 grams
Getting married (homosexual)	600 grams
Telling your partner you love him or her	400 grams
Divorce	700 grams
Jealousy	60 grams
Obsession	500 grams
Writing a love letter	30 grams
Writing a love e-mail	20 grams
Going on a date	200 grams
Group sex/orgy	800 grams

Rest

Seated	7 grams
Reclining with feet up	5 grams
Reclining in fetal position	3 grams
With a week's garbage and unfinished work on the floor	1 gram
Hammock	3 grams
On floor	2 grams
In coffin	2 grams
With no reason to get up	2 grams
Avoiding obligations	5 grams

Business

Make phone call to stockbroker	10 grams
Writing e-mail to stockbroker	7 grams
Returning phone calls	30 grams
Negotiating business deals	100 grams
Initiating business deals	200 grams

Bankruptcy	60 grams
Calling a literary agent	50 grams
Buying a house	100 grams
Having a meeting	75 grams
Applying for a job	100 grams
Opening a business	300 grams
Opening a play	400 grams
Building a house	400 grams
Traveling on business	400 grams
Promotion	500 grams

Sloth Zone Activities

Sleep	0 grams
Nap	Negative 30 grams
Coma	Negative 100 grams
Not moving for twenty-four hours	Negative 50 grams
Hibernation	Negative 20 grams
Achieving numbness	Negative 20 grams
Emotional apathy	Negative 20 grams
Loss of all appetites	Negative 50 grams
Distance from God	Negative 1,000 grams
Rereading this book	Negative 25 grams